Mazes Are Amazing!

By T. A. Parrott

Strategy Focus

As you read, **monitor** how well you follow what happens, and reread to **clarify** anything you don't understand.

 HOUGHTON MIFFLIN   BOSTON

Key Vocabulary

awesome causing a feeling of wonder

convinced made to believe something

disappeared went out of sight

discovered found

incredible hard to believe, amazing

impossible not able to happen

Word Teaser

This word means the opposite of *under*. It's inside a longer word. What is the word? What is the longer word?

Can you use your finger to find your way through this maze?

Not all mazes are on paper. People can walk inside some mazes! This maze is made of tall bushes. It is in a garden in England.

Some people are convinced that this maze is one of the oldest in the world. They're probably right. It was made for a king over 300 years ago.

Some people have turned cornfields into mazes. People look in wonder at this awesome maze made from a cornfield.

People who walk into a maze together may lose each other. Once people take a turn, they can't be seen. But no one has ever just disappeared in the corn!

This maze is made of trees. There are so many
turns that it is almost impossible to follow the path.

Visitors who were lost discovered a tower inside this maze. When they climbed to the top, they were able to see how to get out. Can you find the tower?

This mirror maze in England is an incredible sight. It's hard to believe that every visitor finds the way out!

10

People see themselves at every twist and turn in this mirror maze. Along the way, they hear music and see a beautiful fountain.

Mazes are a fun way to get lost! They really are AMAZING!

NOTE

NOTE

NOTE

Putting Words to Work

1. What is the setting of one of the **incredible** mazes in this book?

2. Has the author **convinced** you that mazes are amazing? Explain your answer.

3. What would you do if your best friend **disappeared** in a garden maze?

4. Why do you think some mazes have tall, **awesome** sides?

5. **PARTNER ACTIVITY:** Think of a word you learned in the book. Explain its meaning to your partner and give an example.

Answer to Word Teaser

disc<u>ove</u>red